THE 3RD DISTRICT SERIES
Official Artbook

S. J. Garrett

DEDICATED WITH LOVE TO ALL THE FANS OF MY DISTRICT. I'M SO GLAD YOU CAME ON THIS JOURNEY WITH ME.

In 2006, I had one of those crazy moments so common to me as an author, where an idea came into my head that was so vivid, it just had to be written. That first incarnation of THE SHAUGHNESSY FILE is not much to speak of, but it held all of the core components that would later create magic as my ability to write and tell stories continued to evolve. After several rewrites, in 2013, THE SHAUGHNESSY FILE was first picked up for publication under my pen name. It republished in 2016 under my real name, and THE CARMICHAEL FILE followed shortly. Later that same year, THE DEASE FILE came out. In May of 2017, THE LUCINO FILE was released, and--finally--after more than a decade of work, the final book, THE TABER FILE, released in August 2017.

The journey you took through those books is one I took alongside you. I laughed when you did, and I cried when you did. Because I am as wholly a photographer as I am an author, I am in the singularly special place to create my own art for my own books. Inside this artbook are the many photos I've taken, along with some behind-the-scenes information, and some special paintings made by the incomparable Dawn Star Wood that literally walked off the pages of my stories! At the very end, you'll find a special bonus District story that was once printed in an anthology and is now here again to be enjoyed.

Welcome to the 3rd District.

The SHAUGHNESSY File

3RD DISTRICT SERIES BOOK ONE

S. J. Garrett

The book that started it all. I had almost as much trouble casting Aenya Shaughnessy as I did getting published in the first place! The wait paid off as Uva Stega, a dear friend, stepped into the role perfectly. She should look familiar to fans of my books: she portrayed Tariah Chronis, too!

THE DANCING PRINCESS

THE DANCING PRINCESS shoot was, easily, one of my most complicated.
I needed a 'club', onlookers, and a magical atmosphere. The club came
courtesy of my living room being walled with cheap black tablecloths (for
real), the onlookers came from assorted friends and family, and the
magical atmosphere came from holiday lights and bubble machines. Here's
a look behind the scenes!

Right: Me on a ladder rigging lights
from the ceiling fan.
Below: The final lighting setup.

Both photos snapped by Dawn,
my accomplice and dear friend.

A light test shot, as well as test of the bubbles. Dawn and her boyfriend were on bubble duty.

Aenya's dress was created by Theresa Vann-Stribling of Monarch Creations, whom you can see in the background of several of these images. All masks were created by Sabrina Weiss of Sapphire Masquerade Designs (who was also an attendee)!

AEYNA SHAUGHNESSY

These images were shot for the re-release
of THE SHAUGHNESSY FILE, which is
why they might seem so new to those
who bought the book in first release!

This photo was meant as an outtake
until I realized how utterly and adorably
Aenya this actually was! So, yes, now
you know what her glasses look like.

The CARMICHAEL File

3RD DISTRICT SERIES BOOK TWO

S.J. Garrett

You know hard it is to find someone who could be mistaken for a real life faerie? Surprisingly hard! Ashley Elizabeth, however, fit the bill to a tee.

A special thanks to J.D. Brown, who is a dear friend and brilliant author within her own right, who gave me the tagline to put on this book.

SNOW WHITE

Ashley did her own makeup, and her lip color played perfect homage to Snow White's classic look.

Gwyn's corset is also a work of Monarch Creations. It was also not as cold during this shoot as it looks. We shivered but did not freeze.

Almost from the moment I met Kristin Marshall during another shoot, I knew I wanted her in my District. I briefly considered her for Aenya, but it turned out that she more truly embodied the spunk and sass of the Paprika Princess Sarah from THE DEASE FILE.

PRINCESS & THE PEA

The fact that Sarah and Sera have the same name is more than a joke for the characters. Both derive from the same Hebrew root meaning 'princess.'

Sarah's gorgeous ginger locks are a wig from EpicCosplay, who is actually the source of nearly every wig I use, and is responsible for all of the locks within this artbook.
Did you know THE DEASE FILE was originally going to have two other stories, and did not have Louise? Her story is a completely original faerie tale I created and decided fit perfectly within the Dease family. The other two who got rejected? Well . . . time may tell just what happens to those . . .

I met Maggie Trevor while doing another shoot for Monarch Creations, and I almost pounced on her to be my Isabelle and Gabrielle Lucino. Imagine my delight when I asked if she thought she could pass for Italian, and she revealed she was in fact half Italian herself! Coincidence? Bite your tongue.

PRINCESS & THE PAUPER

How do you turn one subject into two very different identical women?
Costumes, body language, and a bit of digital magic!

Theresa is another character who appeared late in the ouline, process. I wrote her story before TANGLED came out, and then had to go back to account for it!

They used my frying pan joke before I could . . .

The penultimate magic! A camera on a tripod, stand-in figures, and Maggie's amazing acting give us this moment from the books that could not have existed otherwise.

I had thought finding a faerie would be hard, but finding a woman so beautiful she could make Aphrodite jealous proved even harder! When the dust settled, I had found Emily Labowitch as my perfect Rhianna, and I had also found a wonderful new friend. She really encompassed Rhianna's wisdom and humor all at the same time!

PSYCHE & CUPID

Let's talk about Rhianna's epic hair in this shoot. Jenelle Mullen-Smith is a brilliant stylist and an artist within her own right. When I told her I wanted a modernized version of an Ancient Grecian style--and then handed her this insanely long wig--she stepped up to the task and did not disappoint!

An additional shoutout needs to go to my friend Luna who has become my go-to guru for makeup on shoots, including here for Rhianna.

There are a million little connectors in
the series, but did you catch this one? In
THE DEASE FILE, Brian gives Rhianna a green
dress in Grecian style--and she wears it to the
engagement party in THE LUCINO FILE!

Secret: Look at family tree in THE
TABER FILE that shows the names of
Rhianna and Aaron's twin daughters.
Check out their meaning for more
mythological fun.

It might not immediately show, but a great deal of research went into Psyche and Eros' story to ensure as much historical accuracy as possible. The same happened with Kay's story back in THE SHAUGHNESSY FILE. Even in a world flooded with magic, I wanted to build my world as plausible as I could, and that meant using as many facts as needed to build the scene.

I should probably mention that I made the chiton you see Rhianna wearing. For something so simple, it was an *ursa* to make.

See, because *ursa* means bear in Greek and... oh, nevermind.

The Enforcers' official logo, as designed by Dawn Star Wood.
If you see this on a contract, you can expect something magical to follow.

INSERT IMAGES

The following images are found within the books themselves as the 'cover' to each folder section. I like to imagine these photos are ones Rhianna herself uses to help keep track of her files.

AENYA
THE DANCING PRINCESS

KIENAN
THE NIGHTINGALE

TAEGAN
CINDERELLA

MEL
BEAUTY & THE BEAST

KAY
THE RAVEN

RAYNA
SLEEPING BEAUTY

GWYN
SNOW WHITE

TRAHERN
SEVEN WISHES

JERAN
THE GOLDEN BIRD

CAMERON
PRINCESS & THE PEA

KENNETH
THE MAGIC LAMP

LOUISE
THE WEAVER'S WIFE

TERRA
WILLOW & OAK

ISABELLE & GABRIELLE
PRINCESS & THE PAUPER
STATUES MADE BY INSANELY TALENTED POPGARDEN ON ETSY!

RAFAEL
THE UGLY DUCKLING

THERESA
RAPUNZEL

DAMIAN
THE ENCHANTED FAERIE

PSYCHE
PSYCHE & CUPID

RHIANNA
PSYCHE & CUPID

AARON
JACK & THE BEANSTALK

ELIZABELLE
MY FAIR DRAGON

On the next many pages, you will find the extraordinary work of Dawn Star Wood, who remains one of my most favored collaborators. Her work graces the Descendants series as well, so when I decicded I wanted to actually see Taylor's paintings come to life, well, who ELSE would I have called? Below is one of the idea sketches she sent me early on, and as you can see, it's a work of art in itself!

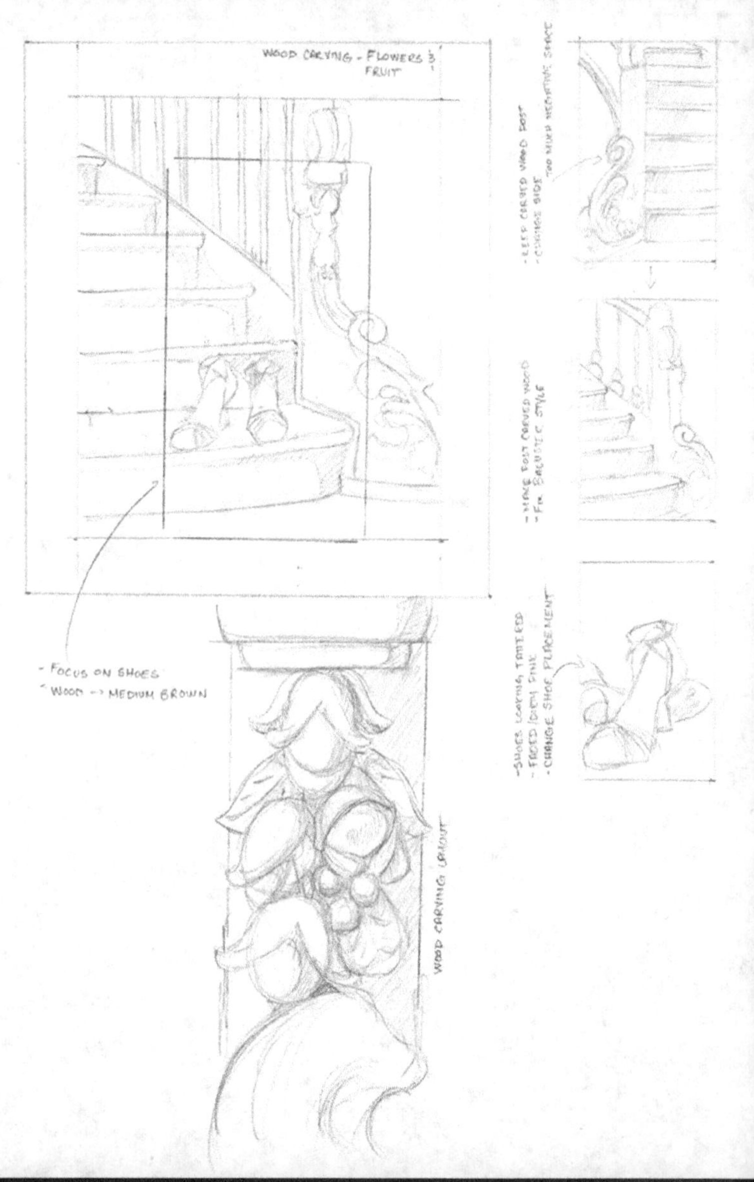

In 2015, I was asked/challenged to write a 5000 word short story to be featured in an anthology that would donate its profits to charity. I took on that challenge, and I decided to write Sullivan Shaughnessy's tale. On the following pages, please enjoy this look into a moment both before and after THE SHAUGHNESSY FILE. Bittersweet though it may be, there is still a happy ending. Love, after all, never truly dies.

Mini Folder
Sullivan

Sullivan Shaughnessy looked out at the audience gathering on both sides of the aisle and felt more than a little nostalgic. The Christmas lights lining the chairs. The glorious trees decorated to the nines in the corners. Beautiful carols being sung, though this time by his daughter-in-law and not his sister. Thirty-four years before, the same scene. The same moment in time. A wedding celebrating love and happy endings. If he had not had his, he wouldn't have been standing there to honor his daughter's.

He tucked his hands into his pockets as he headed back through the winery toward the changing room where Aenya was still getting ready. Eyes watched him wistfully as he went by. Even at almost sixty, he was trim and handsome, and his hair still stubbornly refused to release all of its black color to the silver creeping in.

He knocked briefly on the changing room door and asked, "Can I come in?"

"Of course!" was the response.

He opened the door and felt his heart ache with a blend of pride and sadness. A part of him had always wished to keep his four children *as* children, yet more of him was happy they had found their happy endings and would get to know real joy. "You look beautiful," he said simply as he shut the door behind himself.

Aenya Shaughnessy—soon to be Michaels—turned in a happy circle in front of the mirror. The custom made wedding gown flattered the dancer's tiny form and pale hair, and it was lightweight enough to allow her to move freely and easily. "I feel beautiful! Getting to wear a B. R. Matthews wedding dress down the aisle . . . just, wow! I'm so glad he decided to take pity on me when I begged."

Sullivan had to smile as he sat down on the chaise in the room. "I'm not sure you can call it begging when you cornered him at the Faerie Club and demanded he make you something."

She shot him a grin. "I'm my father's daughter. I know how to get what I want. It was his fault for taking a day off from his shop and coming into my club." She walked over and sat down beside Sullivan. "Dad . . . thank you." She shook her head when he lifted a brow. "For letting me have a Christmas wedding. I know it probably stings a little, because you and Mom were married at one, too."

"In a way," he murmured after a moment, "it helps ease the sting. Full circle, I think." He smiled. "Have I ever told you how I met Sam? It was another holiday party. And, in hindsight, I do think that there might have been some . . . help along the way."

"Was this help four-legged, covered in fur, and possibly working on someone's order?" she asked politely, but with obvious humor.

"Whatever makes you think that?" Matching humor was in his honey colored eyes, so like his daughter's. His eldest son most resembled him, Aenya resembled their mother—though with Sullivan's eyes—and his other two sons had picked up the brown-haired gene that popped up now and then in the Shaughnessy bloodline. Such a fascinating blend of him and Samantha their four children were! "Interested in another faerie tale before I walk you down the aisle?"

Aenya giggled. "You know me. I love a good faerie tale! Is there a contract in yours?"

He grinned a bit. "Conveniently, there is. Let's see, how do they start?"

"Once upon a time, looooong ago . . ."

"Not that long ago, you little hellion."

(Thirty-four years before)

The party had been going on for more than a few hours, and it had yet to be anything more than a smattering of inane small talk, children squealing over excessively cute toys, and the same ten holiday songs on repeat. Sullivan had nothing against Bing Crosby, but if he heard *White Christmas* one more time on the radio, he would lose his mind.

It was Christmas Eve, and there were two hours to go until midnight when everyone would say the obligatory 'Merry Christmas' and disperse to get sleep. Sullivan was there under minor duress; it was a huge company party, and because he was the heir apparent to the family's business, Shaughnessy Corporation, he was expected to attend.

He supposed he ought to feel a little like a prince waiting to inherit a kingdom, but he hardly felt royal when he liked to get dirty, work hard, and was already nagging his mother into letting him do more. The thought made him smile. Perhaps it was a family trait; his mother said she had been the same way in her youth, and it hadn't even been that acceptable for a woman to do so!

In desperate need of fresh air, he headed out through the back of the Glass Shoe Palace and into the elaborately decorated gardens. The Palace was located in the 3rd District within New York City, and it could be rented for events. The staff of the place had gone to town with the winter wonderland theme, with all the cheer and maniacal glee of particularly enthusiastic elves. Then again, perhaps they *were* elves. In the District, anything was possible.

The 3rd District could not be found on maps. Most New Yorkers weren't even wholly sure it existed. Yet, it was said, that the District was the place of magic. Where magic was born. If you were drawn there, then you would find your happy ever after and all your dreams would come true. The residents were whispered about, said to be either gifted or not human, or both. Sullivan thought it a nice tale, and he thought it could very well be true. One of his ancestors had come from the District, and certainly all Shaughnessy children since had been . . . gifted.

He had wandered partway into the garden, and the music was only a faint tinkling of bells. The full moon bathed the landscape in beautiful silvery color. He swung around a corner to find a bench, and instead he found himself face-to-face with a stunningly beautiful young woman. "My apologies," he started to say, only to look again. A slow smile started to cross his face. "Then again . . . maybe I'm not sorry."

Samantha Donohue could only boggle at the young man in front of her. The lethally beautiful smile crossing his face should have had *warning* labels; it seemed unfair to inflict it on helpless maids. She could swear it was some sort of mating call, and her hormones were quite happy to respond! "Uhm. Hello." It was the best she could manage, particularly when she had the absurd urge to say *Take me! I'm single!* "I wasn't watching where I was going. I was just finishing up for the day."

Sullivan took a slight step back to study her again and realized she wore dirty work clothes instead of formal attire. "You work here?"

She smiled. "I alternate between weeding the garden and mopping the floors. I'm just a part-timer. I needed a holiday job, and Enforcers offered me this one. Seemed quite determined to get me under contract." She shook it off and held out a hand. "Samantha Donohue."

Since the same soft hint of a brogue colored her voice as it did his, he was not surprised to hear her name. He also couldn't resist bringing her hand to his lips. "Sullivan Shaughnessy. I'm very happy to meet you, Samantha." He cocked his head. "Sam? Sammy?"

"Sammy to my grandmother only, Sam to anyone who feels like it, and Samantha under normal circumstances." She told herself that he was just being courteous, but she couldn't quite make herself believe it. That smile still tugged at his lips, and there was a look in his honey colored eyes that made her feel like a tasty bunny spotted by a predatory panther. "What brings you out here to the gardens? I thought this was your company's party."

"My company, but not my party." He released her on a shake of his head. "I'd rather have done something more intimate, but I'm not in charge yet. I was coming close to contemplating the murder of Mr. Crosby."

She started laughing. "You and me both!" Liking him as much as she admired him, she offered impulsively, "You are welcome to join me out here. As I said, I was just finishing up. My contract ends at midnight."

He only found it slightly odd that Enforcers would be taking care of contracts for the Palace's help. The Enforcers was one of the biggest companies in the country, and it directly oversaw and protected all members of the District, including those who were temporary. "You're not from the District?"

"Manhattan," she confirmed. Her eyes slowly began to widen as she looked over his shoulder. "Sullivan? Tell me that that belongs to you."

He turned quickly and then let out a relieved breath as he saw the familiar black and gray wolf sitting in the garden path. "She does. Her name is Stormy. She's the family wolf. She's also a courier of sorts." He knelt down and smiled as he rubbed Stormy's ears. "She runs between our company and Enforcers. She's been with the family for long enough that we suspect she's really a good faerie in disguise. Considering Rhianna Taber gave her to us, it's believable."

"Rhianna Taber?" Samantha echoed. "She co-owns Enforcers." She knelt to meet Stormy and found herself looking into yellow eyes too intelligent to belong to an animal. She could believe the good faerie thing, too. "Nice to meet you, Stormy." She straightened again as Sullivan did, and she found herself falling into step beside him as they ambled along behind Stormy down the path. "How old are you?"

"Twenty-four. You?"

"Twenty." She smiled up at him with merry chocolate eyes. "I expected you to be older, considering the things I've heard you do."

He grinned back. "My family is full of overachievers. What can I say? So what do you do when you're not being one of the Palace's helpful little mouses?"

"I am currently studying literature in college. I am the dreaded liberal arts major your family warned you about."

"Will you ruin my favorite books by telling me all the deep meanings the author put in every word, or will you leave my illusions that *Lord of the Rings* could really have happened?"

"My home economics teacher was Gandalf." She nodded firmly when his brows lifted. "Beard and all. And he was fond of saying 'you shall not pass!' I flunked, let's just say. Why do you think I'm in the gardens and not the kitchen? We didn't want to poison anyone."

"We have a chef at home." He contemplated his words when

she looked at him sideways. "That was either a very awkward proposition, or an unintentional proposal. It might also have been a clumsy way of saying 'come over for dinner.' I'm not sure which."

"Is your slip showing, Dr. Freud?"

"And the lace is very drafty." He lifted a brow as Stormy ran off into the bushes. "Well, there she goes again. She's untamable, really." A sudden chill raced down his skin and his head jerked up. "What the hell?" He stopped dead in his tracks as the chill continued to chase. It was not an unfamiliar feeling, unfortunately, and had nothing to do with metaphorical slips. "I didn't know the Palace was haunted." He glanced back at Samantha and found her chewing on her lower lip. "Sam . . ." he said warningly. "Is there something I need to know before we decide whether my proposition and proposal should be on purpose?"

On one hand, it felt gratifying to know she wasn't the only one tripping over her own heart. On the other, she really wouldn't blame him for hiking for the hills if he knew. "It's not the palace," she admitted. She grimaced. "Oh, lord, this will just sound crazy." She huffed a breath out. "I'm the one haunted. There's a banshee affixed to me."

He paused for a moment. "Putting aside the irony of an Irish girl with a banshee affixed to her, *how* did that happen?"

"I don't know!" It was almost a wail. "She just showed up in my room one night and screeched at me! *That* was why I went to Enforcers! I figured that if anyone could give me a crazy idea to get rid of a crazy thing then it had to be the people who protected the place where crazy things happen!"

"Breathe." He caught her shoulders in support, and she slumped against his chest. Unable to resist, uncaring that she was dirty enough to ruin his tuxedo, he tugged her closer. Her arms crept around his waist, and an undeniable sense of *rightness* moved through him. They just . . . belonged together. He could feel it all the way into his soul. "Well, hell," he muttered. "I guess I can no longer regret the party."

She didn't bother to lift her head *or* ask for clarification. "Why did I have to find my dream man while I was being haunted by a banshee? Why couldn't we have just . . . met at college? Or on summer vacation. If she screams and you hear her, it'll paralyze you!"

"That remains to be seen, Sam. I'm not exactly normal myself. I'm trying to remember my lore. Banshees. What's the story again?"

Samantha eased back and reluctantly let go. She was immediately chilled anew, but she had only barely noticed before he removed his jacket and swathed it around her shoulders. Her eyes lingered wistfully on his broad shoulders. His tailored shirt and waistcoat did nothing to disguise that he was built more like a model than a businessman. "There are lots of theories. I think the one I know most is that a banshee is a woman who was driven mad with grief and her screams are wails of anguish."

He raked a hand through his hair in frustration. Yet, strangely, he did not feel at all surprised by this turn of events. His sister and brother had both found their spouses under strange circumstances, and so had his parents. Actually, it almost seemed as if every Shaughnessy had had some sort of odd happening to mark the time they found their soul mate. Why would he be different? "Okay, so we need to help alleviate her grief and she'll leave you alone?"

"I don't know." She fought the bubbling blend of anger and fear churning inside. "And we have until midnight else the Enforcers can't keep me protected any longer."

He looked at the clock on the building. Time had been moving faster than he had expected. In the time he had gone from bored senseless to finding love at first sight, an hour had passed. "Well, we're going to have to play by ear then, as the banshee is definitely approaching. I can feel her." He paused for a moment and then turned, caught Samantha's shoulders, and tugged her up so that he could kiss her. It was brief, but by no means light, and when he let her go again, neither of them could breathe properly. "Just in case," he managed to say huskily.

"I'm not complaining," she said a bit dazedly. "Wow. I'd like to accept your proposition. Just throwing that out there."

A low and mournful cry lifted on the air and banished the sultry mood. The grayed and wispy figure of a woman began to form in the moonlight. She could have been pretty if her face had not been twisted into a grotesque mask from grief and fury. Her hair stood on end around her head, and her bloodshot eyes did not look wholly sane. Tears ceaselessly fell down her pale cheeks. Even slightly translucent in form, some details could be seen in her clothes that implied her death had happened centuries before.

She opened her mouth and let out a scream of such force that it caused a shockwave. It knocked Sullivan and Samantha alike back down the path, and they tumbled many feet before rolling to a stop. Samantha recovered first and managed to get back up to her knees despite her now aching body. She crawled over to Sullivan, terrified that he had been paralyzed, but his eyes opened when she touched his face. "Sullivan?" she whispered.

"Ouch." He gingerly sat up. "My head is ringing, and I feel a bit like I'm moving in molasses, but I don't think she did permanent damage." He hastily grabbed Samantha's wrist when she would have stood. "Stay down! We have a shorter distance to fall if we stay low!" He shook his head a bit to help clear the ringing and then looked closer at the banshee. His body tensed. "Sam. I know her."

"What?! How?!"

"There's a painting of her in my family's home in Ireland. Been there for a few hundred years, since even before we came to America in the 1800s. I think . . . I think she is one of my ancestors."

"That'd be one hell of a coincidence!"

"If that's what you want to call it." He carefully got up to his feet and kept an arm in front of Samantha when she stood as well. "You're Brigit, aren't you?" he asked the banshee with as much calm as he could. "You married my many greats grandfather. You were part of my family." He found a smile. "Shaughnessys need family. Always have. Always have so much love to give. But there was an accident, and my grandfather died. You were driven mad and drowned yourself in the lake."

The banshee let out another scream that again knocked the

couple down. Samantha was again the first to raise to her knees, but this time, Sullivan couldn't manage it. Even with a high resistance to the banshee's wail, he was not outright immune. Try as he might, he could not get up again.

Samantha remained kneeling beside him as she shot Brigit a vicious look. "Don't do to me what happened to you!" she shouted. "I just found him! Why would you do this?! Why let your grief consume you? You can't pass on to be with him if you are like this! You could have spent these few hundred years in the field of forever and instead you've been haunting people! Why me? Because you could see I was like you? Because you somehow knew I would be with Sullivan?"

Brigit's face began to change as the mask slipped. The fury began to ebb and leave only the grief. Her eyes cleared and looked anew at the scene before her, and fresh tears welled. "What have I done?" Her voice, raspy and torn from too many decades of bitter screams, still carried a beautiful melody of her homeland not far removed from Sullivan's own subtle accent. "What have I done?" She buried her face in her hands. "The gods took him from me too soon!"

"And you abandoned your children!" Samantha shot at her. "So what if your time was short? You were still happy for the time you had! You could have endured. You could have honored his memory and then joined him after death! Instead, you made him suffer on the other side, unable to see you!"

Brigit slowly lifted her hand, and a smile both sad and accepting crossed her face. "I cannot argue." Her hair settled around her shoulders where it belonged as she drifted down closer. "I saw you. I saw me in you. In my rage, I did not want you to have what I could not. I am sorry." She touched her eyes with her fingers and gathered her tears. Tenderly she smoothed them across Sullivan's face. "My tears shall remove what I have done." She looked at Samantha with sudden seriousness. "Your future is like mine, but not like mine. Cherish what I did not."

"We will," Samantha promised. She felt Sullivan move and

looked down to see him carefully sitting up. She lent him her strength as well, and her lips trembled as she tried to smile at him. "I think everything is okay now."

"I was listening." He looked up at Brigit and smiled for her. "Can you move on now?"

"I think . . . I can. I can hear him calling my name." She closed her eyes as she floated up higher in the air. "He waits in the field for me." She opened her eyes and smiled then, truly, naturally, and with love. "You'll have four."

"Four?" Samantha echoed. "Four what?" she demanded of Sullivan.

He coughed. "Kids, I think."

She blinked and then considered it for a moment. "Alright," she decided. "I could handle that."

Brigit lifted a hand in soft farewell and faded away into little bits of dust that dissolved in the moonlight. Sullivan and Samantha were left in a suddenly quiet garden while Christmas carols continued to play in the distant background. The air had warmed a bit back to its normal winter bite, and all was peaceful.

They looked at each other for a moment and then began laughing. Sullivan's pristine tuxedo had been thoroughly ruined. He was covered in just as much dirt as Samantha, and she was even filthier than she had begun the whole ordeal. They were both slightly bloodied in places as well, where small stones had gouged flesh. "Why couldn't this have happened while it was snowing?" she asked ruefully. "A white Christmas would have made the landings less painful. Colder, maybe, but less painful."

Sullivan got to his feet carefully and tugged her up as well. "And maybe they'd have played that damn song far less." He drew a deep breath of the cold air and then smiled as he saw something fluttering down. "Better late than never?"

She looked up as well and discovered that clouds had consumed the sky entirely, and snow had begun to fall. "Oh, very funny, nature." She sighed deeply. "Well, at least I'm no longer cursed by a banshee. That's a positive. And I suppose I was lucky you knew her. Does this mean you see ghosts?"

He slid his arms around her waist to bring her closer. "It does," he said gravely. "Since we are apparently supposed to have four kids together, I don't suppose we could just skip the proposition and go right to the proposal? I've decided that I think that was what I was trying to say earlier."

She rose up to wrap her arms around his neck and keep them on eye level. Happiness had begun to bubble inside her with a force she had not imagined possible. "I feel it only fair to warn you that I have a terrible temper. We might fight a lot."

"I do too. I don't mind."

"I'm a restless sleeper."

"I'll just readjust each time you kick me." He was smiling.

She was, too. "And I think I might just love you forever, Sullivan Shaughnessy."

"Conveniently, I think I might just love you forever as well, Samantha Donohue." He looked up as the clock began to toll midnight, and happy cheers could be heard from the ballroom. "Merry Christmas, Sam."

"Merry Christmas, Sullivan." She sighed contentedly as he kissed her again and this time lingered. When they finally eased apart, she murmured huskily, "Take me home. We can shower, snuggle under the covers, and then take advantage of that chef in the morning. Or are you required to stay out the party?"

He scooped her up into his arms just to make her laugh. "I think they'll give me a pass this time." He headed for the garden exit but then stopped and looked back. Stormy was once more on the path, but this time walking away with some sort of contract in her mouth. Sullivan could just make out the word 'Complete' across it, and he smiled. Content, he turned again and headed through the falling snow. For as long as he and Samantha might get, they would treasure every moment.

(Present)

Aenya felt her lips tremble a little as she looked at her father.

"You could have had longer without me."

"But my life would have been so much more boring without you." Sullivan pressed a kiss to her forehead. "You will always be my baby, Aenya."

"Even if I give you a grandbaby?" she teased.

He paused. "Is that imminent?" he asked carefully.

"Let's just say that I have a *great* Christmas gift for Hiro." She laughed as he hugged her again. "Don't blab! Go get in place. I have to finish my makeup and then I'll join you." She kissed his cheek. "I love you, Dad."

"I love you, too, baby." He stood and then left the changing room. As he stepped into the hall, he became aware of the other person present. He said nothing initially as his daughter-in-law walked beside him, and then he asked, "Yes?"

"I wanted to say I'm sorry," Audra Shaughnessy admitted in a low voice. "For your short happy ending. Not all faerie tales are sweet. Some are bittersweet."

He stopped and turned to look in her darkened yellow eyes. "Audra," he said gently, "I understand destiny. And I will always be truly, deeply, grateful for the true happiness I felt for those short years. We got sixteen years. I am honored for them." He patted her on the cheek. "Go find Mel and cherish your own happiness."

"If you insist."

He watched her head down the hall and then headed to the closed double doors that would open onto the aisle. He was only there for a moment before he felt a soft warmth in the air. Slender translucent arms coiled around his shoulders. He could not feel them, but he could see them. "Without your presence, perhaps I may have gone Brigit's route," he murmured.

Samantha smiled and pressed her cheek to his. "We knew our time would be short, Sullivan. I am lonely without you, too. This can be enough until your time is done."

He did not turn to look at her. "I still miss your terrible cooking and the way you'd throw off the covers at night."

"Someday." She closed her eyes. "Someday we'll be together

in the field of forever. Until then, I'm always by your side." She smiled as she began to disappear. "Merry Christmas, Sullivan."

"Merry Christmas, Sam." He turned at a step and found Aenya approaching. He offered his arm on a smile. "Let's get you married. And maybe someday, my next grandchild can be married on Christmas, too."

"A new family tradition?" she teased.

"Better than banshees, isn't it?"

"Definitely better than banshees."

Sullivan was still smiling as he escorted her down the aisle and passed her into Hiro's care. Though he sat alone with his sons and daughters-in-law in the front row, he knew he was not truly alone. Samantha's death would always hurt. He would always miss the touch of her hand and scent of her skin. Still long to snuggle under the covers every Christmas and talk about anything and everything. Yet she was still there. When he needed her, he could see her. Until that day when they met in the field of forever, he could continue to live not just for their children, but for himself. That was the promise they had made.

Though their happy ending had been bittersweet, he focused on the sweet, and not the bitter. It had been *happy*, and that was all that mattered.

What could there be possibly left to share with everyone? How about an unexpected gift?

On the next few pages, you will find photographs taken by Ronni Mae Knepp--photos taken of Dazzle! That's right, Ronni made Dazzle from clay and then took photos of her in case she did not survive the shipping to me across country! Ronni is a brilliant photographer within her own right, and a wonderful friend and fan of the series. I am blown away by how amazing she made my lil' dragon genie look. I'm also blown away by the eerieness of the fact that Ronni, on her own, bought the little lamp you see Dazzle wrapped around, without realizing that it was SAME lamp used in the insert photo from THE DEASE FILE.

We were already convinced we may be twins separated at birth. This did not help matters.

And here, at last, we have come to the end. The end of the artbook, and the end of the District series.

Or is it?

Even I don't always know what the future holds--that would be Rhianna's job--but I do know that there were many faerie tales that did not make the final cut in the books. That there are many other faerie tales, new and old, that might just have a place inside our District. Who knows? Someday we might return again to that little den of magic where the River Styx got stuck. Until then, keep falling in love, and never ever stop believing in happy ever after.

Stacy J Garnett

Stacy J. Garrett was made in England but born in Sacramento, California, and like the redwoods of the state, her roots have dug deep. Her destiny as a bard was somewhat inevitable. Little else can explain how she constantly told her mother tall tales so outlandish that she couldn't even get grounded for them. Her mother and grandmother had her reading by age three, and that love of a good story propelled her through so many books that Scholastic Books gave her a medal. A love of worlds created by others eventually brought out the desire to create her own, and she has never looked back.

Stacy has seen both good and evil in her life, and her stories, like life, have no half measures. Even in a fantasy world of dragons and faeries, even in a modern city where magic abounds, she knows that the constants of real emotion never change. Dreams come true, love can be found at first sight, princesses can rescue their princes, and maybe there really can be happily ever after. Her happy endings never come without cost, though, for she truly believes we can't appreciate the good and the joy without the bad and the pain along the way.

Her current haunt is a comfy house in her beloved Sacramento where she wrangles four feline fur-kids and consumes peppermints like mana in order to balance a calendar filled with more creative venues than a sane person should realistically undertake. If she's not chained to her desk, she's stomping through the scenery in search of equally fantastical photographs.

www.ingramcontent.com/pod-product-compliance
Lightning Source LLC
Chambersburg PA
CBHW071008120726
47910CB00004B/1439